a treasury of
animal stories
& rhymes

A catalogue record for this book is available from the British Library

Published by Ladybird Books Ltd
27 Wrights Lane London W8 5TZ
A Penguin Company
© LADYBIRD BOOKS LTD MCMXCIX
Stories in this book were previously published by Ladybird Books Ltd
in the *Two Minute Tales* series.
LADYBIRD and the device of a Ladybird are trademarks of Ladybird Books Ltd

a treasury of
animal stories
& rhymes

Contents

Bunny Tales
by Nicola Baxter
illustrated by Steve Smallman

Kitten Tales
by Joan Stimson
illustrated by Tony Kenyon

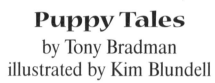

Puppy Tales

by Tony Bradman
illustrated by Kim Blundell

Bunny
Tales

Contents

The Rainbow Rabbits

"Who's got my SOCKS?" cried Mr Rabbit one morning. "Just wait until I find out which one of you naughty little bunnies has got them. Now then, Bayleaf, show me your FEET!"

But the little rabbit just giggled. "I'm not Bayleaf, Dad," he said innocently. "I'm Bluebell. And these aren't YOUR socks, they're Hazel's. And Hazel is wearing Scarlet's socks. And Scarlet is wearing Snowdrop's socks. And Rosebud isn't wearing any socks at all. And..."

14

"Stop!" cried Mr Rabbit. "You're making my ears spin." He peered closely at the little bunny in front of him. "Are you SURE you're not Bayleaf? No? Well never mind. The point is that everything is in a MUDDLE. No one knows who's wearing what, and I still haven't found my SOCKS! There's only one answer to a mess like this–we need a SYSTEM."

Mrs Rabbit sighed. She remembered her husband's PATENT IMPROVED CARROT COOKING SYSTEM–the steam had peeled off all the wallpaper–and as for his WATER-SAVING EAR-WASHING SYSTEM–her ears had lost their wiggle for WEEKS!

15

Before long the floor was tail-deep in paper. "Don't stand on those charts!" cried Mr Rabbit, waving his crayons. "Now, everybody stand still and listen! My new system is based on COLOUR CO-ORDINATION! And," he added modestly, "it's brilliant! What do you think?"

"It's brilliant!" said Mrs Rabbit faintly.

And in a few days Mr Rabbit's system was in operation. Little Scarlet was dressed from paws to ears all in red. Primrose was all in yellow. You can guess what happened to Bayleaf, Snowdrop, Hazel, Bluebell and Rosebud!

16

17

At first the seven little bunnies rather liked looking different, but pretty soon they started to complain.

"I don't LIKE brown," said Hazel. "I want a tee-shirt like Bluebell's!"

"I'm never going to get dressed again if I have to wear horrible GREEN!" wailed Bayleaf.

Mrs Rabbit could hardly think straight with all the complaining; whereas Mr Rabbit insisted that, with a few minor adjustments, everything would be fine.

He set to work again with his famous crayons. But at the end of the day he accidentally left the crayons in his shirt pocket and then put the shirt in the washing machine with all the children's clothes.

When Mrs Rabbit took the washing out of the machine next morning, she laughed so loud that the little rabbits came running. "What's the matter, Mum?" they asked.

Mrs Rabbit choked and sniffled. "I don't want to hear one more word about... ho ho ho... your clothes," she giggled. "Your father has... hee hee hee... invented a new system called... ha ha ha... the **IMPROVED** COLOUR CO-ORDINATION SYSTEM – and we're ALL going to be using it!"

The little rabbits loved their multi-coloured clothes.

"It was time for – hh-hmm! – PHASE TWO of my System," said Mr Rabbit, looking aimlessly at the ceiling.

Another
story
tomorrow.

21

Slippy and the Skaters

There was once a bunny called Cowslip who was very clumsy. She bumped into furniture; she dropped her toast on the floor – jam side down – and she tripped over her own feet.

When Cowslip poured herself a drink, her mum would say, "Give that to me, Slippy. I'LL carry it into the dining room. We don't want MORE milk in the pot plants, do we?"

Cowslip didn't mean to be careless. It was just that she didn't think about what she was doing. And her mind was always on something else.

At playgroup the little bunnies ran round the room to music.

Hoppity, skippety, JUMP!
Hoppity, skippety, JUMP!
Hoppity, skippety, BUMP!

Yes, that was Cowslip. She'd noticed a spider high up on the ceiling and had forgotten to jump.

It seemed that hardly a day went by without Cowslip colliding into one of her friends or spilling her food – OR without someone telling her to concentrate and THINK about what she was doing.

One winter the water in
the village pond froze so
hard that it was safe to
skate on. All the little
bunnies, and some of
the big ones as well, whizzed
and swooped across the ice.
Cowslip went along too, and started to
put on her skates.

"Oh Slippy, PLEASE don't come on the
ice!" shouted her brother. "You're sure to
knock everyone over!"

"Perhaps you'd better just sit quietly on
the bank and think, Slippy," advised her
mum, who was practising her famous
double-axel bunny-loop.

25

So Cowslip sat down on the bank and enjoyed watching her mum. She was a brilliant skater.

Soon the little bunny's mind moved on to other things. She noticed the way the ducks slithered and slipped on the ice, and wondered why they didn't wear skates; she noticed that old Bunny Hopkins was wearing odd socks and that his jacket didn't quite fit; she noticed that the ice was melting in the middle of the pond...

WHAT? "STOP!" cried Cowslip. "The ice is melting!"

In only a minute or two all the skaters were safely off the ice. Now they could see the growing hole in the middle, too.

"Well done, Slippy," said her mum. "You were the only one thinking about the really important things. My double-axel bunny-loop and your brothers and sisters might never have been seen again!"

Another story tomorrow.

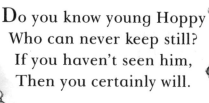

The Dancing Bunny

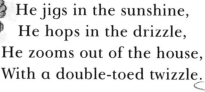

Do you know young Hoppy
Who can never keep still?
If you haven't seen him,
Then you certainly will.

He jigs in the sunshine,
He hops in the drizzle,
He zooms out of the house,
With a double-toed twizzle.

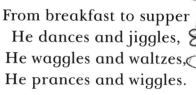

From breakfast to supper
He dances and jiggles,
He waggles and waltzes,
He prances and wiggles.

And when sleepy Hoppy
Is tucked up in bed,
He's dancing the foxtrot
Inside his own head!

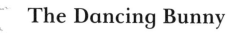

Turn over for another bunny rhyme.

Visiting Wizard Whee

Five little bunnies
Knocking on the wizard's door;
One was rather nervous,
So then there were four!

Four little bunnies
Said hello to Wizard Whee;
One went home with hiccups
So then there were three!

Three little bunnies
Found some magic spells to do;
But they muddled up the words,
So then there were two!

Two little bunnies
Having lots of wizard fun;
One found a magic hat,
So then there was one!

One little bunny
Wished his friends were back again;
The naughty wizard said a spell,
And then there were ten!

Turn over for another bunny rhyme.

31

Mrs Bunny Had Twins...

What wonderful news!
But what names would she choose?
So many relatives
Had their own views.

Said old uncle Boris,
"Have you thought of Horace?
And Doris? Or Morris?
Or Norris? Or... BORIS?"

Smiled grandmother Connie,
"Dear, what about Ronnie?
And Bonnie? Or Jonnie?
Or Lonnie? Or... CONNIE?"

Cried young cousin Harry,
"But what about Barry?
And Carrie? Or Larry?
Or Gary? Or… HARRY?"

Laughed poor Mrs Bunny,
"Here's Sonny. Here's Honey.
For names don't sound funny,
When they rhyme with… BUNNY!"

Another story tomorrow.

The Trouble With Babies

One day Timmy's mum sat him on her knee. "Timmy," she said, "soon you are going to have some little brothers and sisters to play with. Won't that be nice?"

Timmy was very excited. He was tired of playing all by himself and he could hardly wait for the new bunnies to be born. He tidied up his toy box and started to think of good games he could play with his brothers and sisters. He lined up all his cars and his big yellow tractor under the table. "This can be Timmy's Garage," he thought. "The little bunnies can drive my cars and I will be Chief Mechanic."

34

"Come and see your new brothers and sisters!" said Timmy's dad a few days later. Mum was sitting up in bed holding four little bundles. Timmy tip-toed forward.

"But they're tiny!" he squeaked in surprise. They certainly didn't look big enough to drive his big yellow tractor.

"They'll grow very fast," laughed Mum.

But things didn't get better next day or the day after that. The babies didn't grow very fast at all. They seemed to be asleep nearly all the time – and they wouldn't even open their eyes!

35

A few weeks later the little bunnies started to smile and gurgle. Timmy waited until his mum was out of the room.

"It's all right," he whispered to his brothers and sisters. "She's not here. You can stop pretending now and talk to me."

But the little bunnies just smiled and gurgled again.

"Come and see my garage," said Timmy. But the little bunnies didn't seem at all interested.

Mum found Timmy looking sad. "My new brothers and sisters don't like me," he said. "They won't talk to me and they don't want to share my toys."

"But Timmy," said his mum, "that's because they're only a few weeks old, and you are a BIG bunny now. They have a lot to learn, and YOU can help me to teach them to do all the things that you can do."

So Timmy put away his cars and his big yellow tractor. "Little bunnies are not ready to play with big toys yet. They have a lot to learn," he announced. Then he piled some cushions and his picture books under the table. "This is Timmy's School," he said. "And I am the Baby Bunny Teacher!"

Another story tomorrow.

39

Everard's Ears

Once there was a bunny called Everard who had extra-large ears.

"Everard, your ears are ENORMOUS!" laughed his friends Basil and Beech.

Everard's ears started drooping, and he looked very unhappy.

"It's all right! You just haven't grown into your ears yet, son," said Everard's dad. "And, who knows, one day you may find they come in useful."

But Everard couldn't think of a single reason why big ears would ever be of any use at all. And it seemed his friends would NEVER stop teasing him.

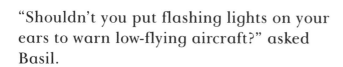

"Shouldn't you put flashing lights on your ears to warn low-flying aircraft?" asked Basil.

"No wonder there's a hole in the ozone layer," giggled Beech.

Everard's ears drooped down even further.

"Ears up, son," said Everard's dad. "Any rabbit can have ORDINARY ears, but you're my EXTRAORDINARY Everard. And don't you forget it!"

41

Now there was a big cabbage field
nearby, and whenever there was washing
up or bedroom tidying to be done,
Everard, Basil and Beech would hop off
into the field to hide. They would sit
among the huge cabbages, nibble leaves
or play games – and wait until they
thought it was safe to go home.

One afternoon in the cabbage field, Beech started laughing. "Everard!" he giggled, holding two big cabbage leaves above his head. "What do these remind you of?"

Everard didn't think it was funny. He chased Beech through the cabbages until they were both exhausted.

"Stop!" puffed Basil, trailing along behind. "Where are we?" The cabbages had grown so high that the bunnies couldn't see which way to go.

After hours of running in all directions, the three bunnies were near to tears. "We'll be here for EVER!" said Beech. "I'm sorry, Everard, it's all my fault!"

43

The frightened little bunnies flopped down among the cabbages. "No one will ever find us," sobbed Basil.

"But, if we ever do get out, we promise never to make fun of you-know-what again, Everard!"

A few minutes later they heard a cheery voice nearby. "Come on, boys," said Everard's dad. "I'll show you the way home. It's lucky I reached you before it got dark."

"How ever did you find us?" asked Beech, as they all tramped home together.

Everard's dad looked down at his son's ears waving above the cabbages. He gave Everard a big wink. "Let's just say I had EXTRAORDINARY good luck," he said.

Another
story
tomorrow.

45

The Princess Bunny

ONe night Holly's babysitter read her a bedtime story about a princess who was kept prisoner by a dragon. A brave prince rescued the princess and she lived happily ever after.

"I'd like to be a princess," said Holly to her little brother Ben. "But I'd quite like to do the brave rescuing too."

"Huh," said Ben sleepily. "I'd rather be a dragon."

A few days later, as Holly took a short-cut across the farmyard, she nearly hopped into a wire fence.

"That wasn't here before," she muttered. She was just about to go on when she saw a beautiful bunny inside the fence.

"She must be a princess!" gasped Holly. The new rabbit had long white fur and a tiny pink nose.

47

Holly didn't think twice. "Don't worry," she cried. "It's Holly here. I'll rescue you!" She found a little gate in the fence, pushed open the bolt, and hopped inside.

"Delighted to meet you. I'm Florabell," said the bunny. "What…?"

"Just follow me," said Holly. "There's no time to lose!"

So the princess bunny hopped into the farmyard. "I'm not sure…" she said.

"COME ON!" cried Holly. "Can't you hop any faster?" And she scampered into the next-door meadow.

"I'm not used to hopping over FIELDS," complained Florabell. And she flopped down and wouldn't go any further.

"It's very kind of you to visit," she said, "although I don't really like hopping games. Anyway I think I must get back now. It's time for my dinner."

"But I'm rescuing you!" wailed Holly.

"Well, it's been very nice to meet you," said Florabell. "But I've got a very cosy house of my own and a little boy brings me lovely things to eat. He'd be so sad if I got lost. You must drop round for another delightful chat some time. Goodbye!" And Florabell hopped cheerfully home.

Next time the babysitter came she asked if Holly and Ben would like the story about the Princess again.

"No thank you," said Holly. "We'd like a story with lots of dragons and no princesses AT ALL!"

50

The Tale
of the
Bunny
Princess

Turn over
for another
bunny rhyme.

51

Belinda's Bedtime

When it was time to go to bed,
Belinda Bunny always said,
"I'm just not ready yet to go.
I'm not a baby now you know!"

One night her mother counted ten
And sat down in her chair again.
"This fuss is more than I can take.
All right, Belinda, stay awake!"

This was a very big surprise!
Belinda yawned and rubbed her eyes.
Now that her mum had let her stay,
She really felt too tired to play.

A minute passed – it seemed like ten!
Belinda's voice was heard again.
"I think it's time to go to bed,
I'm only little still," she said.

The end.

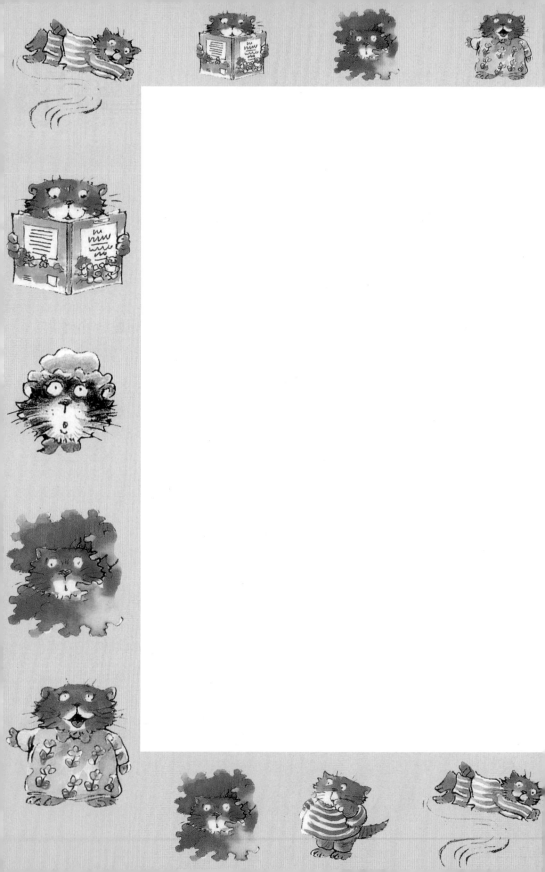

Kitten
Tales

Contents

The Roly Poly Kitten

Once upon a time there was a Roly Poly Kitten. He was friendly, he was cheerful and, although he didn't know it, he was just a little plump.

One day it rained so hard that the Roly Poly Kitten had to stay indoors. All morning he chased his brothers and sister.

At last lunch-time came. "Now, sit down," said Dad, "and eat nicely."

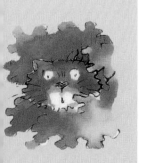

The Roly Poly Kitten bounced up to his place and tucked in. But the other kittens grumbled at him.

"Move over," cried one. "You're taking up all the room!"

"Hey!" squealed another, "you're sitting on my tail."

But, loudest of all, yelled the smallest kitten.

"Go away!" she cried. "You're a FAT KITTEN and I can't reach the food."

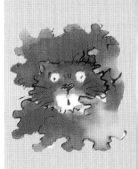

59

"WHOOOOOOSH!" The Roly Poly Kitten ran right out of the house and hid under a hedge.

"I'm fat! I'm fat!" he sniffed. "And nobody likes me." Then he took a deep breath and tried to look thinner. But that only gave him hiccups.

Back home, Dad was worried. "We shall have to make a search party," he announced.

"Ooooh, I LOVE parties," squealed the smallest kitten.

But Dad looked stern. "What I mean," he explained, "is that we must find your brother."

Eventually the kittens
reached the hedge
where the Roly Poly
Kitten was hiding.
And at the same time
a stranger arrived.

"I'm looking for my son," Dad told her.
"Now, let me describe him."

"Oh no!" thought the Roly Poly Kitten.
He didn't want to hear how fat he was.
But his family shouted so loudly that he
didn't miss a word:

"He's friendly." "He's cheerful." "He's
handsome." "He's strong."

"He's…" the smallest kitten thought
carefully, "CUDDLY!" she squealed.

"That's right," smiled Dad. "He's a very
special kitten indeed."

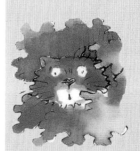

63

The Roly Poly Kitten was too surprised to speak.

"Wherever can he be?" wondered his family. And in the end they went to look at home.

Inside all was still and quiet. But not for long.

"WHOOOOOOSH!" The Roly Poly Kitten sprang out of his hiding place.

"I feel friendly," he cried. "I feel cheerful. I feel handsome. I feel strong. I feel cuddly."

"But, most of all," decided the Roly Poly Kitten, "I feel... HUNGRY!"

Another
story
tomorrow.

Don't Tell Tiger!

The farm kittens were planning a picnic.

"Let's eat at the old barn," they agreed, "outside if it's fine and inside if it's wet."

On the way to the barn the kittens met a cow.

"What ARE you doing?" she mooed.

"We're going on a picnic," said the first kitten. "But don't tell Tiger! He's such a ROUGH kitten."

Next the kittens met a pig.

"What ARE you doing?" he grunted.

"We're going on a picnic," replied the second kitten. "But don't tell Tiger! He's such a NOISY kitten."

Next the kittens met a sheep.

"What ARE you doing?" she bleated.

"We're going on a picnic," said the third kitten. "But don't tell Tiger! He WILL speak with his MOUTH FULL."

Next the kittens met a donkey.

"What ARE you doing?" she brayed.

"We're going on a picnic," announced the fourth kitten. "But don't tell Tiger! He tells such DREADFUL jokes."

At last the kittens reached the old barn. Tiger was nowhere in sight.

But, suddenly, "YAP, YAP, YAP, YAP!" Bully, the farm dog, appeared.

"Oh goodie," he growled, "a picnic!" And he was just about to eat it.

"What ARE you doing?" boomed a big, rough voice. It wasn't a very clear voice, because someone had his mouth full.

"Oh no!" cried Bully. "It's Tiger. He's been having a snack in the barn. And now he's going to tell me one of his DREADFUL jokes."

Bully shot off in a panic. But the kittens looked at each other and blushed. Then they looked down at their saved picnic.

"I know," they all cried together... "LET'S TELL TIGER!"

Another story tomorrow.

71

Catnaps

You can take one on the bus top,
You can take one in a store,
You can take one at the fun fair,
And then come back for more.

You can take one in the car wash,
You can take one if you chew,
You can take one with your teddy bear,
(I hope there's room for two!).

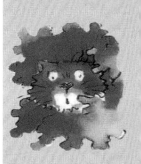

You can take one after playgroup,
You can take one while you grow,
You can take one when it's time to wash,
Your mum will never know.

You can take one at the dentist,
You can catnap AND still peep,
But stay awake to read these rhymes,
Then snuggle down to SLEEP!

Turn over
for another
kitten rhyme.

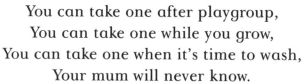

73

The Kitten and the Kangaroo

The kitten and the kangaroo
Were bored and wondered what to do;
"I know," said Kanga, "take a ride,
Here's my pouch, just hop inside."

The kitten took a mighty leap;
"I say," she said, "you're mighty steep;"
"Come on," said Kanga, "grab a paw,
I'll take you on a guided tour."

The twosome bounced across the town;
"Gee-up," cried Kitten, "don't slow
down;"
But Kanga groaned, "I've had enough,
I'm high on bounce and low on puff."

"But I've NO pouch," the kitten cried,
"To give my weary friend a ride;"
She thought and sighed and
thought some more;
Then rushed off to the Superstore.

The boss was kind. He heard her plan,
"I'd like to help you if I can;
Here's a trolley, take good care,
I think your friend could fit in there."

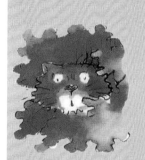

So Kanga rode back home in style;
While Kitten pushed and
gave a smile,
"I may be small, but you
will find
I'll NEVER leave a
friend behind."

Turn over for another kitten rhyme.

75

Tabitha Walker

Tabitha Walker's
A terrible talker;
She talks ALL the time;
It's time someone taught her
To go a bit slower,
Before she gets worse;
Tabitha's talking's a TERRIBLE curse!

Tabitha Walker's
A terrible talker;
She talks ALL the time;
It's time someone bought her
Some candy or carrot
To chew on instead;
Tabitha's talking's a pain in the head!

Tabitha Walker's
A terrible talker;
She talks ALL the time;
We ought to report her;
But, wait, there's a silence;
WhatEVER's the matter?
WOW! Tabitha Walker's run out of chatter!

Another
story
tomorrow.

Let Me Hear You Purr

Tom and Tess were practising their purr. They wanted to collect some money for the kitten hospital. Tom knocked on Auntie Flo's door.

"We're helping sick kittens," he explained. "And the more we purr, the more you can pay us!"

"What a lovely idea!" exclaimed Auntie Flo. "Now, let me hear you purr."

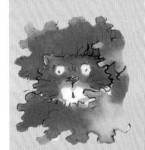

Tom and Tess took a deep breath. They began to purr their heads off. It was amazing. Somehow two purrs together sounded more like twenty!

"STOP IT!" cried Auntie Flo, all of a fluster. "You'll wake the baby. Now, here's some money for those sick kittens."

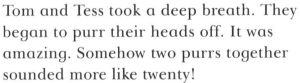

Next Tess knocked on Cousin Clive's door. "We're doing a sponsored purr," she told him.

Clive thought he was too busy to help. But then he agreed. "Okay, let me hear you purr."

Tom and Tess got started right away.

"STOP IT!" cried Clive in a panic.

"I can't hear the television. Now, here's my pocket money."

"BANG, CRASH, BANG!" Tom and Tess hammered on Grandma Gossip's door.

"Well I never, fancy that, such a kind thought," rattled Grandma Gossip. "Now, let me hear you purr."

But, as soon as Tom and Tess began, there was a frightened squawk from inside the house.

"Now you've done it–scared the parrot!" cried Grandma Gossip. "STOP THAT RACKET!"

And she tipped up her piggy bank.

By the time Tom and Tess reached home, Mum was on the telephone. At last she finished her call.

"That was Grandma Gossip," she explained, "…AND Cousin Clive AND Auntie Flo. And we've ALL come to the same decision:

"Next time you collect money for the hospital, let us hear you… *whisper*!"

Another
story
tomorrow.

83

The Kitten
Who Wanted the Sun

"What's that lovely red ball?" asked Jessica. And she pointed to the top of the hill.

"Why," laughed Mum, "that's the sun. And it's just going down for the day."

"I WANT IT!" announced Jessica, "...all for myself."

"Don't be silly," said Mum firmly. "The sun is for sharing. Without it nothing could grow and we should all FREEZE!"

That night Jessica tossed and turned. She couldn't get the bright red ball out of her mind. So, early next morning, she set off to find it.

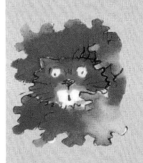

At first the journey was fun. Jessica could see the sun quite clearly. And she purred as she padded towards it.

But then Jessica began to worry.

"However fast I go," she said, puzzled, "the sun doesn't come any nearer."

86

And then, to Jessica's horror, the sun disappeared completely!

Suddenly Jessica wanted to go home.

"Silly old red ball," she repeated to herself until... high in a tree, she saw it.

"Wow!" cried Jessica. "It's the sun. And I'm going to have it all to myself."

Jessica scrambled up the branches as fast as her legs could carry her. She reached forward with her paws... AND her claws.

"BANG!" There was a huge explosion and Jessica fell to the bottom of the tree. She picked herself up and ran blindly towards home.

"BANG!" There was a smaller explosion.

"THERE you are!" cried Mum. "You nearly bowled me over."

"Oh Mum," sobbed Jessica. "I've burst the sun and we're all going to FREEZE!"

Mum held Jessica close. Then she looked down at her paws. They were covered in something red and rubbery.

Mum smiled. "No kitten can reach the sun," she said. "What you burst was a lost balloon. The sun is still safe and, look, it's just coming from behind a cloud."

Suddenly Jessica felt warm and happy all over. She purred as she padded home beside Mum, watching the sun getting brighter and brighter.

Another story tomorrow.

Ten Go to Kitten Camp

Mrs Grey was beginning to regret it.

She had taken NINE kittens to camp and they were behaving badly.

"Now, settle down," cried Mrs Grey. "We've all had a busy day and it's time to get some sleep."

"SWISH, SWOOSH!" One of the kittens flicked his tail and tickled his neighbour. Suddenly the whole tent was flicking and giggling.

"Now really!" cried Mrs Grey.

But, just as the kittens stopped giggling...

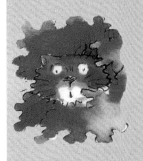

"SWOOSH, SWISH!" Another kitten waved her tail in the moonlight.

"WHOOOO, WHOOOO!" she moaned. Strange shadows appeared on the side of the tent.

"I am the Kitten Camp Ghost," she wailed.

And very soon the tent was filled with waving tails and screams.

"Stop it at once!" cried Mrs Grey.

But, just as all was calm…

"SWISH, SWOOSH!" The kitten with the longest tail threw it across the tent like a lasso. Then she wrapped the end tightly round Mrs Grey's whiskers. And tweaked them!

"OUCH!" cried Mrs Grey. "That does it."

Nine kittens held their breath and their tails. Then they heard a terrible sound.

93

"SNIP, SNIP!"
Mrs Grey's scissors gleamed in the moonlight.

"You w-w-wouldn't," stuttered nine squeaky voices.

"Oh yes I would," announced Mrs Grey. And she started to cut a large piece of bandage. This was an EMERGENCY. "Look what I found in the First Aid Box!" she beamed.

Then quick as a flash, Mrs Grey fastened each kitten's tail to the inside of the tent. "NOW, settle down and get some sleep!"

"But we're not sleepy," wailed the kittens. As they swished their tails once more, Mrs Grey's emergency plan started to work—one after another, the kittens rocked themselves to sleep.

Just as everywhere went silent…

"SWISH! SWOOSH!" But this time it was only the sound of Mrs Grey's tail as SHE settled down to sleep!

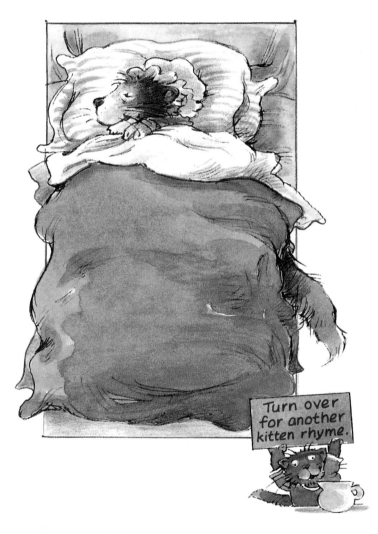

Turn over for another kitten rhyme.

Howard's Dream

When Howard went to sleep at night,
He'd dream that he could fly,
He'd take off from his comfy bed,
And purr across the sky.

He'd wave to kittens far below,
And point up to the stars,
"Just watch me kittens, while you can,
I'm on my way to Mars!"

Now Howard knew a trick or two,
He liked to dive and spin,
And while his friends all hid their eyes,
He'd give a cheerful grin.

"There's nothing to it," Howard cried,
    "Just watch this victory roll,"
But all the kittens squealed with fright,
    As Howard... lost control.

Nine Howard lives seemed lost in one,
    As down and down he sped,
But Howard woke up just in time...
    In Howard's comfy bed.

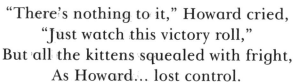

The end.

Puppy
Tales

Contents

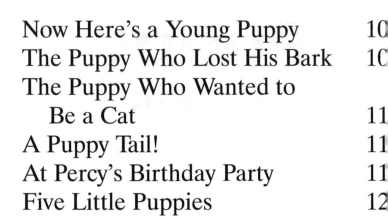

Now Here's a Young Puppy

Now here's a young puppy
Who looks very sweet,
With his long velvet ears
And over-sized feet;

With his little white teeth
And eyes deeply brown,
His tail always wagging,
A patch on his crown.

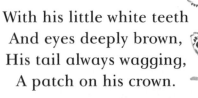

But he's full of mischief,
Of trouble and fun,
As these tales will tell you,
Once you have begun.

So you'll soon discover
What all puppies do;
They're nice, and they're naughty…
They sound just like you!

Turn over
for another
story.

The Puppy
Who Lost His Bark

Patch was a young puppy who couldn't stop barking.

It was the first thing he did when he woke up every morning, and the last thing he did every night. He went, "WOOF-WOOF-WOOF!" all day long. Sometimes he even barked in his sleep.

"Do you have to be so noisy, Patch?" his mum often said. Patch would simply go "WOOF!" and nod his head.

"I wish you were quieter, Patch," his dad would sigh.

"WOOF-WOOF-WOOF!" would be Patch's reply.

Then one fateful day, something
AMAZING happened. Patch woke up
in his basket, opened his mouth...
and nothing came out! His mum and dad
could hardly believe their big, floppy ears.

Patch had lost his bark!

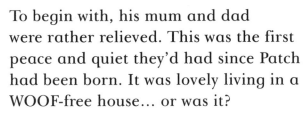

He was as
surprised as they
were. He kept
opening his
mouth and trying
to bark, but he
couldn't raise a
single, tiny yap.
Patch was completely
and utterly… WOOF-less.

To begin with, his mum and dad
were rather relieved. This was the first
peace and quiet they'd had since Patch
had been born. It was lovely living in a
WOOF-free house… or was it?

After a while they began to worry.

"Do you feel all right, Patch?" his mum
said.

Patch looked up at her and shook his head.

"There, there, Patch," said his dad.
"Don't cry."

A little whimper was Patch's only reply.

Patch felt hot, and his throat was sore, and soon the doctor was at the door. Patch had a temperature, he'd caught a nasty bug. He had to have some medicine and stay cuddled up snug.

The next morning, Patch was MUCH better. He woke up in his basket, opened his mouth… and went "YAP!" Then he went, "YAP-YAP-YAP!" and followed that with a… "WOOF-WOOF-WOOF!"

His mum and dad winced. They realised they were probably in for a very noisy day. But they looked at Patch and thought, "Actually we wouldn't want to have him… any other way!"

Another story tomorrow.

The Puppy
Who Wanted to Be a Cat

Life seemed far too busy for Penny the puppy. There was always something her parents wanted her to do, and she was fed up with it. So one day, Penny decided to be... a cat.

"Cats can do whatever they like," Penny said to her brother and sister. "I mean, just look at Ginger!"

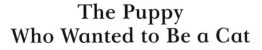

Penny and her family shared the house with Ginger the cat. He did an awful lot of dozing, and was never, ever in a hurry.

"You're a dog," said Penny's brother. "You can't be a cat."

"Oh, can't I?" said Penny. "We'll soon see about that!"

From then on, Penny copied everything Ginger did. She walked like a cat, stretched out on the rug like a cat, and even tried to miaow like a cat, although that was quite hard.

And when her parents told her to do something, she said, "I'm sorry, I can't do that. I'm a cat!"

As you can imagine, after a while, this started to drive her parents CRAZY. So they came up with a plan...

The next morning Penny got a surprise. At breakfast, her brother's bowl was full of lovely, chunky dog food, and so was her sister's. But Penny's contained something rather strange.

"What's THIS?" said Penny, sniffing at it.

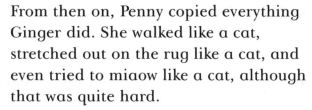

"Well, it seems you're a cat now," said her mother, "so we thought you ought to have... CAT FOOD for your meals."

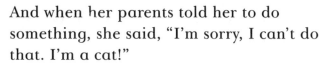

Suddenly Penny wasn't sure being a cat was such a good idea.

How could Ginger eat this disgusting stuff? It was SO yucky…

The rest of the family burst out laughing at the look on Penny's face. Penny laughed too when her father took away the bowl with the cat food in it, and produced a proper breakfast.

And from then on Penny was a puppy
again. At least she was – until she saw a
bird flying through the sky...

"Don't be absurd," said her sister. "You
can't be a bird!"

But Penny's parents wouldn't put
anything past her...

And neither
would I!

Another story
tomorrow.

115

A Puppy Tail!

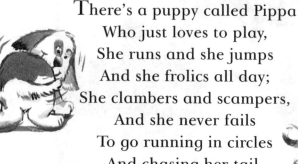

There's a puppy called Pippa
Who just loves to play,
She runs and she jumps
And she frolics all day;
She clambers and scampers,
And she never fails
To go running in circles
And chasing her tail.

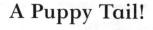

Round like a whirlwind,
Round in a blur,
A small, dashing ball
Of teeth, paws and fur;
Round till she falls
And can chase it no more,
And lies pooped and panting,
Collapsed on the floor.

But Pippa's a puppy
Who just can't be beat;
Which means in a minute
She's back on her feet;
She KNOWS she can do it,
She's SURE she won't fail...
That's why she's a puppy
Who chases her tail!

Turn over
for another
puppy rhyme.

At Percy's Birthday Party

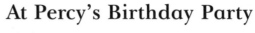

Percy the puppy is one today,
And he's having a party – hip hooray!
The doorbell's ringing, so let them in,
Now is the time for the fun to begin.

Come one, come all
And have a ball
At Percy's birthday party!

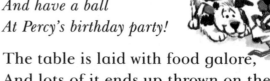

The table is laid with food galore,
And lots of it ends up thrown on the floor;
The cake is delicious, soft and sweet...
Just right for treading in with your feet!

Come one, come all...

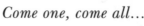

Next Percy says,
"It's time for some games,
Like *Musical Chairs* and *Guessing the Names*,
And *Jumping to Catch a Floating Balloon*,
And *Forming a Queue to Howl at the Moon*."

Come one, come all...

Percy, alas, begins to play rough;
And Mum is soon saying,
  "Enough is enough!"
Percy's in danger of losing a friend...
Thank goodness his party
  has come to an end!

Come one, come all...

Percy the puppy
  has gone off to bed;
(Mum's sitting downstairs
  with an aching head);
He's had a great party – hip hooray!
It really has been a wonderful day!

Come one, come all
And have a ball
At Percy's birthday party!

Turn over
for another
puppy rhyme.

Five Little Puppies

Five little puppies
Having lots of fun,
Along came a little girl
And took Number One.

Four little puppies
Playing peek-a-boo,
Along came a little boy
And took Number Two.

120

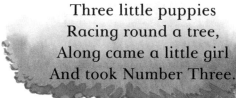

Three little puppies
Racing round a tree,
Along came a little girl
And took Number Three.

Two little puppies
Rolling on the floor,
Along came a little boy,
And took Number Four.

One little puppy
Waiting on his own,
That's when I came along...
And took MY puppy home.

Another
Story tomorrow.

121

Good Boy, Pickle!

Pickle the puppy was beginning to think he would never be able to do ANYTHING right. He tried his very best to be good, but whatever he did seemed to turn out wrong.

This morning, for instance, Pickle woke up in his basket, and set off to start the day in his favourite way... with something yummy to eat from his big bowl in the kitchen.

"Good boy, Pickle!" Tom said, and patted his head.

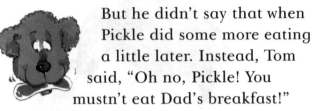

But he didn't say that when Pickle did some more eating a little later. Instead, Tom said, "Oh no, Pickle! You mustn't eat Dad's breakfast!"

Next, Tom and his family took Pickle for a long walk in the park. Pickle really enjoyed himself, and when he made a puddle by a big tree, everyone seemed to think it was wonderful.

"Good boy, Pickle!" Tom said, and patted his head.

But he didn't say that when Pickle made another puddle a little later. Instead, Tom said, "Oh no, Pickle! You mustn't do puddles there!"

At home, Pickle went to the corner where he kept the old bone Tom had given him. Pickle loved chewing, and after a few minutes of crunching and cracking he forgot his troubles.

"Good boy, Pickle!" Tom said, and patted his head.

125

But he didn't say that when Pickle did some more chewing a little later. Instead, Tom said, "Oh no, Pickle! You mustn't chew the table leg! You're a naughty, naughty puppy!"

Tom picked Pickle up and held him close to his face. Tom looked cross… but then Pickle suddenly thought of what he should do. He stuck out his tongue – and licked Tom's nose!

"Good boy, Pickle!" said Tom, giggling in between the slurps. "But you'll have to stop now. You're tickling, Pickle!"

But Pickle just kept on licking. He wasn't about to give up doing the only thing he seemed to have got right all day…

Another story tomorrow.

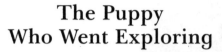

The Puppy Who Went Exploring

Prudence the puppy was very excited. It had been such a thrilling day! She had started it living in one place, and now she was living somewhere completely different.

Her family had moved into a new house. Prudence couldn't wait to go exploring, even though she'd be going on her own. Her mum and dad and sisters all said they had too much to do.

"See you later, everybody," she said, and trotted off.

"Don't get into any mischief, now," her dad called out.

"Really," thought Prudence, "as if I would!"

129

Prudence went through the nearest door, and found herself approaching a cave full of interesting things. She snuffled inside it for a while, but then the things attacked her.

"Yikes!" said Prudence, "I'm off!"

She skidded into a nearby room, where she saw a strange box thing standing in the corner. She stood on her hind legs and sniffed at it... and suddenly it made a very loud noise!

"Yikes!" said Prudence, "I'm off!"

She scampered up the stairs and dashed into another room. There she found a big, puffy thing that was just right for biting and tugging at... but it tried to smother her!

"Yikes!" said Prudence, "I'm off!"

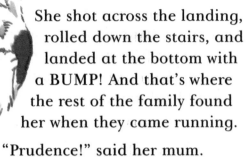

She shot across the landing, rolled down the stairs, and landed at the bottom with a BUMP! And that's where the rest of the family found her when they came running.

"Prudence!" said her mum. "What DO you think you're up to?"

"Quick, everybody," said Prudence breathlessly. "Let's get out of here before it's too late…"

When they'd stopped laughing, Prudence's family showed her round the house. She discovered the cave was a broom cupboard, the box thing was a television, and the puffy thing a duvet.

To make her feel more cheerful, her dad found her a bone. And next time she went exploring–she didn't go alone!

Another story tomorrow.

133

My Puppy Loves His Basket

My puppy loves his basket,
He loves his blanket, too,
He loves to eat his dinner,
He loves a shoe to chew;
He loves his tummy tickled,
He loves to play with toys,
He loves some rough and tumble,
He loves to make a noise;
He loves to go out walking,
He loves his favourite tree;
He also loves a person...
I'm glad to say it's ME!

Turn over for another puppy rhyme.

Polly

Polly was a puppy,
Small and trim and neat,
A puppy with a hobby…
Polly liked to eat.
Her tummy always rumbled,
It couldn't get enough;
Polly had to keep it filled
With lots of tasty stuff.

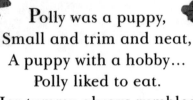

Beef and crunchy biscuits,
Sausages and lamb,
Chunks of red salami,
Mincemeat, rabbit, ham,
Fish and chips and bacon,
Chocolate bars and cheese,
Apple cores and marrowbones,
Dundee cake and peas.

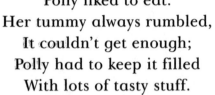

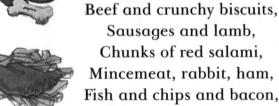

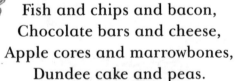

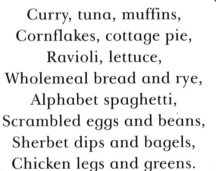

Polly liked to root around
In dustbins for odd scraps,
And sit beneath the table
With her snout in people's laps,
Waiting for a present,
Or some food to simply fall;
It didn't matter how it came,
Polly ate it all.

Curry, tuna, muffins,
Cornflakes, cottage pie,
Ravioli, lettuce,
Wholemeal bread and rye,
Alphabet spaghetti,
Scrambled eggs and beans,
Sherbet dips and bagels,
Chicken legs and greens.

137

Polly kept on guzzling,
She ate and ate and ate,
And pretty soon she wasn't small,
Polly put on weight;
She grew in all directions,
An inch a day at least;
But did that stop her eating?
No! Her appetite INCREASED!

Liver, yoghourt, salad,
Burgers and French fries,
Jacket spuds and chilli,
Steak and kidney pies,
Doughnuts, Danish pastries,
Any kind of fish,
Apricots and jelly,
Quiches from the dish.

Polly WAS a puppy,
But now she's very big;
She uses loads of energy;
And still eats like a pig.
Her tummy's always rumbling,
Demanding tasty stuff;
It doesn't matter what she eats,
She'll never get enough!

Carrots, onions, cherries,
Samosas, Christmas cakes,
Cauliflower, rhubarb,
Mangoes, strawberry shakes,
Coffee, toffee, mustard,
Custard piping hot;
Whatever food that she can find...
Polly eats the lot!

Turn over for another puppy rhyme.

A Puppy Goes Walking

There once was a puppy
Who hung round the door,
Leaping and yapping
And scratching the floor;
I knew what he wanted
Though he couldn't talk;
My puppy was desperate...
     To go for a walk!

It took just a second
To clip on his lead,
And then he set off
At astonishing speed;
He zig-zagged all over
The pavement as well,
His snout twitching wildly
At each brand new smell.

He stared in amazement
At cars roaring by,
And hated the wet stuff
That fell from the sky;
He started to shiver,
He slowed to a crawl...
And soon his small paws
Were not moving at all.

I picked up my puppy
And he licked my cheek;
I knew what he wanted
Though he couldn't speak;
Home, and some dinner,
And plenty of rest...
A walk is exciting,
But snoozing is best!

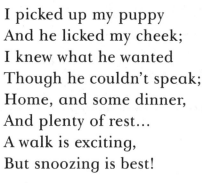

The end.

141